THIS BOOK BELONGS TO
M. A. McLEAN

HAIRY TALES
and
NURSERY CRIMES

D0043744

More poetry in Young Lions

MICHAEL ROSEN

HAIRY TALES
and
NURSERY CRIMES

Illustrated by
ALAN BAKER

YOUNG LIONS

First published in Great Britain 1985
by André Deutsch Limited
First published in Young Lions 1987
Eighth impression September 1992

Young Lions is an imprint of
the Children's Division, part of
HarperCollins Publishers Ltd,
77–85 Fulham Palace Road,
Hammersmith, London W6 8JB

Text copyright © 1985 Michael Rosen
Illustrations copyright © 1985 Alan Baker

Printed and bound in Great Britain by
HarperCollins Manufacturing, Glasgow

Conditions of Sale
This book is sold subject to the condition
that it shall not, by way of trade or otherwise,
be lent, re-sold, hired out or otherwise circulated
without the publisher's prior consent in any form of
binding or cover other than that in which it is
published and without a similar condition
including this condition being imposed
on the subsequent purchaser.

Dedication

For Joefish and Eddily
and all young peep-hole
who breed books
and like to laugh tumshimes

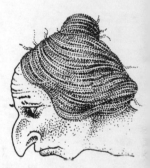

Nursery Rhymes

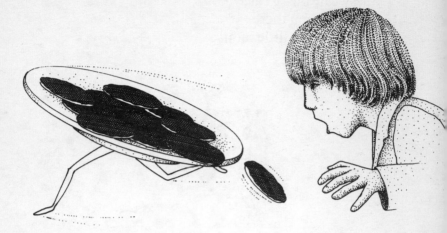

Hey diddle, diddle,
The cat and the fiddle,
The cow jumped over the moon;
The little dog laughed
To see such fun,
And the dish ran away with the chocolate biscuits.

Pussy cat, pussy cat,
Where have you been?
I've been to London
To look at the bean.
Pussy cat, pussy cat,
What did you there?
I frightened a little mouse
Under her hair.

Jack and the Tinstalk

Once upon a tyre there lived a boy called Jack who
lived with his mother in a little mouse.
His mother was very poor and all she had was one
old car.
Now, one day, Jack's mother got up and there
wasn't a scrap of food left in the whole mouse.
So she said to Jack,
"Jack, get up, we've got to sell the car."
So Jack got up and took the car to market to sell it.
When he got there, he went up to a man and said,
"Excuse me, would you bike to lie a car?"
"Yes," said the man
"Cow much?" said Jack.
"A bag of magic tins," said the man.
So Jack gave the man the car and the man gave Jack
the bag of magic tins.

When Jack got back to his mother's mouse, his
mother said,
"Did you sell the car?"
And Jack said, "Yes mump."
"Can I have the money, then?" she said,
and Jack handed over the bag of magic tins.

"What's this?" she said.

"Magic Tins," said Jack.

"Tins? Tins?" she said.

"They're no good. We can't eat tins. Oh dear, what are we going to glue now?"

At that she threw the magic tins out of the windbag into the garden.

Then she sent Jack upstairs to bread.

In the morning, when Jack broke up, he looked out of the windbag and there was a great big tinstalk growing where his mother had thrown the tins.

When Jack saw that, he thought,

"I would like to climb that tinstalk."

So he climbed out of his breadroom and up the tinstalk.

Up, up, up until he got to the pop. And when he got there, there in front of him was a huge Car-Sale.

So he walked up to the gates of the Car-Sale and there was a great big woman standing there who said,

"You can come in, if you like; but look out because my husbad will be back soon and he is a Gi-ant and if he sees you he'll wobble you up for his dinner."

And then the woman gave Jack some bed and butter and a cup of pee.

Just then there was an awful sound.

"Quick," said the woman. "You must hide, Here comes my husbad."

And she helped Jack into the cupboard under the stink.

Then the Gi-ant came in. He was singing:

"Fee fi fo fum

I smell the blood of an English bum."

"Well there's nothing here," said the woman, and so
the Gi-ant sat down to eat a huge plate of fish and
ships.

Then the Gi-ant said to the woman,
"I want to count my honey. Where's my honey?"
And so the woman went off and got the Gi-ant's
honey bags.

And then the Gi-ant sat down and counted his honey
bags till he got so tired he went to sheep.

At that, Jack came from out of the cupboard under
the stink and he upped and grabbed some of those
honey bags and off he went as fast as his eggs could
carry him, and on down the tinstalk.

When he got back to his mother's mouse, he said,
"Mump, Mump, look what I've got," and he
showed her the honey bags.

She was very pleased and put half in the fridge and
half in the sneezer.

The next day when Jack broke up he climbed up the
tinstalk once again.
And when he got to the Car-sale gates, the woman
said to Jack,
"Go away. My husbad will be back soon and if he
finds you he will heat you up."
But Jack said, "Fleas, let me in." And they did.
And then the woman sat Jack down and gave him
something to eat – a glass of ginger beard and a great
big chocolate kick.

16

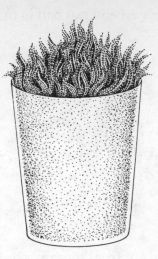

Just then they heard the Gi-ant coming.
Jack rushed to the cupboard under the stink.
And in came the Gi-ant:
"Fee fi fo fum
I smell the blood of an English bum."
"Well there's nothing here," said the woman.
And so the Gi-ant sat down to eat a huge plate of
potatoes, brussel snouts, and a huge leg of cork.

After a while he said, "Bring me my magic hen that
lays golden legs."
So off went the woman to get it.
And when she brought it back the Gi-ant said,
"Lay."
And the magic hen laid a golden leg. The Gi-ant
then ate it.
After this, the Gi-ant got a bit tired and went to
sheep.

17

Then Jack came out from the cupboard under the stink and he upped and grabbed the magic hen and off he went as fast as his eggs could carry him, and on down the tinstalk.

"Mother, Mother," he said, "look what I've got."
And he put the magic hen down.
"Lay," he said, and the hen laid a golden leg.
And everytime they ever wanted a golden leg, all
they had to do was say, "Lay."

But Jack wanted more, so the next day he climbed
up the tinstalk once again.
When he got to the gates of the Car-sale, this time he
waited.

So the woman came out to clean the cars and as she
went to fill a bucket of daughter, Jack crept in
through the door and hid in the cupboard under the
stink.

19

Not long after, in came the woman, and not long
after that in came the Gi-ant.
"Fee fi fo fum
I smell the blood of an English bum.
Be it alive or be it dead
I'll grind its bones to make my bed."

20

"Well, there's nothing here," said the woman.
But the Gi-ant didn't believe her. "It's here
somewhere," he said, and off he went round the
kitchen. He cooked everywhere for it. But the one
place he didn't cook was the cupboard under the
stink.

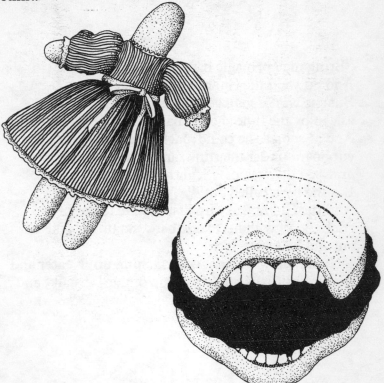

So then the Gi-ant sat down to eat.
He ate a huge plate of sausage dolls, legs and bacon,
scream cake, and he drank a huge jug of orange
wash.
When he had finished, he said,

"Bring me my magic bark."
And off went the Gi-ant's wife to get it.
But she was so long getting it, the Gi-ant was fast
asleep by the time she got back with it.
And as soon as he could, Jack crept out of the
cupboard under the stink, and he upped and
grabbed the magic bark and away he ran.
But the bark called out, "Woof, help, woof."
And the Gi-ant woke up just in time to see Jack
running off with his magic bark. So up gets the Gi-
ant and he's after Jack.
Jack ran but the Gi-ant was catching up. Nearer and
nearer until Jack got to the pop of the Tinstalk, and
down he climbed.

Then the Gi-ant got to the pop of the tinstalk, too; at
first he didn't feel like climbing down, but the bark
called out,
"Woof, help, woof," and so the Gi-ant started
coming down the tinstalk after Jack.
And the whole tinstalk was shaking from the weight
of the Gi-ant, but the Gi-ant was getting nearer and
nearer but Jack got to the ground first.
And he ran up to his mother and he said,
"Mother, Mother, get the snacks."
And his mother ran out of the mouse with the snacks
in her hand.
A plate of sand-witches.

So Jack took the sand-witches and they cast an evil
smell on the Gi-ant. And the Gi-ant roared out,
"Fee fi fo fum
I smell."
So Jack's mother ran inside to get some nice smelly
stuff to squirt all over the plate but she did better
than that, she picked up the fly killer instead and she

squirted that all over the Gi-ant. Down crashed the Gi-ant and the tinstalk on top of him. So that was the end of the Gi-ant.

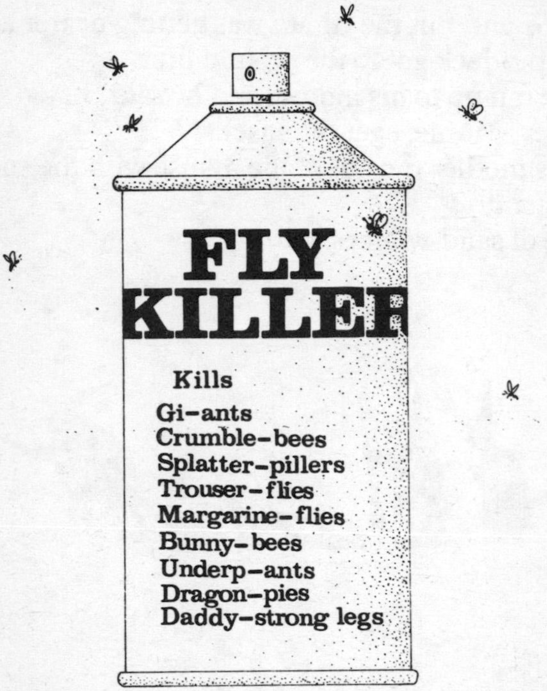

FLY KILLER

Kills

Gi-ants
Crumble-bees
Splatter-pillers
Trouser-flies
Margarine-flies
Bunny-bees
Underp-ants
Dragon-pies
Daddy-strong legs

So Jack and his mother and the sand-witches ate up the honey bags, the magic hen laid golden legs, the magic bark barked and they all lived hoppily ever laughter.

25

Simple Simon met a pieman
Going to the fair;
Said Simple Simon to the pieman
"What have you got there?"
Said the pieman to Simple Simon
"I've got a load of pies."
Said Simple Simon to the pieman,
"Ugh – they're all covered in flies."

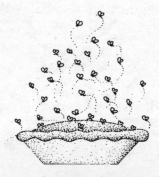

Old Mother Hubbard
Went to the cupboard,
To fetch her poor dog a bone;
When she got there
the cupboard was bare
And so the poor dog had a moan.

Handsel and Gristle

Once a plum a time, in the middle of a forest, there lived a poor woodnutter and his woof. They lived in a little wooden sausage with their two children, Handsel and Gristle. The one was called Handsel because he had huge hands and the other was called Gristle because it was all gristly.

One day the woodnutter came home and he says: "I've been nutting wood all day long but I couldn't sell Lenny."
(No one knew who Lenny was, no one asked him and no one has ever found out).
Anyway, that night the children went to bed with puffin to eat.

Downstairs, the woodnutter and woof talked.
The woodnutter says, "How can we feed the
children? They've gone to bed with puffin to eat
again."

"Quite," says woof, "that's what I was stinking.
There's only one thing we *can* do – take them off to
the forest and leave them there."

"But that would be terrible," said the woodnutter.
"They might die of gold, they'd sneeze to death out
there. Or they might starve and die of Star Station."

"Well," said woof, "they might die of Star Station
here. We've got no money because you went nutting
wood all day and couldn't sell Lenny."

(There's Lenny again.)

29

What the woodnutter and woof didn't know, was that Handsel and Gristle were still a cake and they could hear everything the woodnutter and woof were sighing.

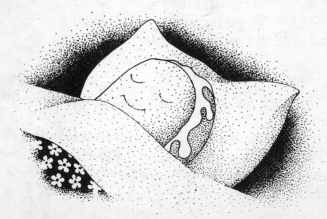

Later that night, when everybun was in bed, asweep, Handsel crept downstairs, out into the garden and filled his rockets full of phones and then crept back to bed.

The next day, Woof said, "Right, children, today we're all going to the forest to nut wood."
They all left the little wooden sausage and off they went.
As they walked along woof noticed that Handsel kept stopping.
"Keep up, Handsel," woof said. What woof didn't notice was that Handsel was taking the phones out of his rocket and dropping them on the ground.

They walked and walked and walked until in the end they hopped.
"Well," said woof, "you two stay here, we've got to go off and nut some wood." And off they went.
Handsel and Gristle played together for a bit till they felt so tired they lay down and fell asweep.

When they poke up it was bark and they were all abone.
Gristle didn't know where it was, but Handsel said, "Don't worry, leave it to me," and there, shining in the spoon-light were the phones all the way back comb.

31

When they got back, their father was very pleased to see them but woof was very cross.
"Oh, you wicked children, why did you sweep so wrong in the forest. We thought you'd never get back comb."

That night the woodnutter and woof sat and talked again.
"Well," said woof, "we'll just have to try again. We'll take them a long way, bleep into the forest."

Upstairs Handsel and Gristle were still a cake and they could fear everything their father and woof were sighing.

So later, when everybun was in bed, Handsel staired down crept. But this time the sausage door was locked. He couldn't get out. Sadly he went back to bed.

Curly in the morning, woof got the two children up. "Right, we're all going off to the forest again to nut wood. Here's some bread for you to eat when we get there."
And off they went.

As they walked along, Handsel broke off little boots of bread and dropped them on the ground behind them.
"Handsel," said his father, "Why do you keep shopping?"
"I'm not shopping," said Handsel. "We haven't got any money – you couldn't sell Lenny, remember?"
"Who's Lenny?" said the wood nutter.
"Keep up Handsel," said woof.

They went bleeper and bleeper into the forest to a place they had never seen before or five.
"We're just going off to nut some wood. We'll come and get you before it gets bark," said woof. And off they went.

Handsel and Gristle played for a pile and then, when they smelt tired, they went to sweep. When they poke up it was bark.
"Don't worry, Gristle," said Handsel, "all we have to do is follow the boots of bread."
"What boots? What bread?" said Gristle.

"I croak up my bread into little boots," said
Handsel, "and all we have to do is follow the
creadbums."

But when they started to look for the creadbums,
there weren't Lenny.
(Hallo Lenny)

You see all the birds of the forest had eaten them. So
they walked and walked, lay down, walked and
walked and walked – but they were lost. They
walked some more and suddenly they came upon a
little house.

The whales of the house were made of gingerbread, the wind-nose were made of sugar and the tyres on the roof were made of chocolate.

Handsel and Gristle were so hungry that they ran up to the house and started to break off bits of the chocolate tyres and sugar wind-nose.

Then all of a sudden, a little old ladle came out of the house.
"Oh, what dear little children, come in, come in. You look so hungry. I'll give you something to beat."
She took them inside and gave them a huge pile of cancakes.

Handsel and Gristle thought they were very lucky – what they didn't know was that the little old ladle was really a wicked itch – a wicked itch that lay in wait for children. The itch then killed them to eat.

When Handsel and Gristle finished their cancakes,
the itch took hold of Handsel's hand (which was
very easy considering how big it was) and before he
knew what had happened, the itch threw him into a
rage in the corner of the room.

"Aha, I'm a wicked itch," said the little old ladle,
"and you'll stay in that rage till you're nice and cat.
And as for you," said the itch to Gristle, 'you can
fleep the swore."
"Who swore?" said Gristle. "Not me."
"Shuttup," said the itch, "or I'll eat your eyes."

Now, this itch couldn't see very well. In fact, most
itches can't see very well and Gristle noticed this.
Every day, the itch watched Handsel's rage and the
itch said,
"Hold out your finger, boy. I want to know if you're
getting cat."
"Are we getting a cat?" said Gristle.
"Shuttup," said the itch "or I'll eat your nose."

It was about this time that Gristle told Handsel that
the itch couldn't see. (Which Handsel knew all along
because all the itches he knew just itched and
nothing much else.) Anyway, because of this,
Handsel didn't hold out his finger for the itch, he
yelled out a bone instead.

"Not ready yet," the itch said.
Well, four weeks passed by and the itch said, "I
can't wait this pong. You're cat enough for me."
"He's nothing like a cat," said Gristle.
"Shuttup," said the itch, "or I'll eat your lips."
Then the itch told Gristle to fill a kettle of water and
light the fire in the gloven. When Gristle got back,
the itch said,

"Is the fire ready?"
"I don't know," said Gristle.
"Stupiddle thing," said the itch. "I have to do
everyping round here."

Then the wicked itch went right up to the gloven door, but Gristle was just behind and Gristle gave the itch one pig push; the itch went flying into the gloven; Gristle slammed the door, and that was the end of the wicked itch.

Then Gristle ran over to Handsel and got him out of his rage.
"Handsel, we're free," said Gristle.
"Three?" said Handsel. "There's only two of us now you've got rid of the itch."
But they were so happy they hugged and missed and danced and sank all round the room.

Then they filled their rockets full of bits of chocolate tyres, gingerbread whales and sugar wind-nose and ran back through the forest to the woodnutter's little sausage.

When he saw Handsel and Gristle, he was overjointed. Woof was dead by now, so Handsel and Gristle and the old woodnutter lived afferly ever harpy.
(And they never did sell Lenny)

Hush-a-bye, gravy, on the tree top,
When the wind blows the ladle will rock;
When the bough breaks the ladle will fall,
Down will come gravy, ladle and all.

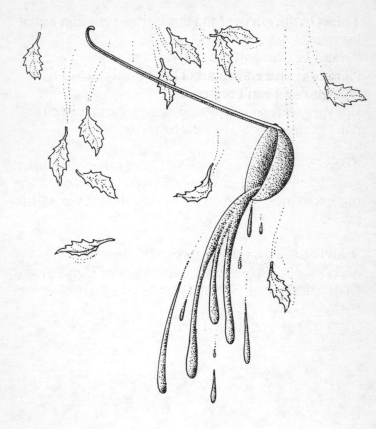

Yankee Doodle came to town
Riding on a yeti;
He stuck a feather in his cap
And called it fresh spaghetti.

Thirty days hath September,
And the rest I can't remember.

Goldisocks and the Wee Bears

Once a popper time there were wee bears. And they all lived tobother in a house in a porridge.
There was great bug bear, there was muddled eyes bear, and there was shiny wee bear. One morning they all got up and made themselves some polish.

Then they poured it out into some holes and went off
into the porridge to let the polish cool down.
A little whale later, a little ghoul called Goldisocks
came along. She walked up to the house and looked
in. She was very hungry so she went up to the table
where the holes full of polish were.

Thirst of all she went up to the great bug bear's
polish in the great bug holes and she tried it. "O-o-h,
much too hot," she said.
Then she went up to the muddled eyes bear's polish
in the muddled eyes holes, "O-o-h, much too old,"
she said.
And then she went up to the shiny wee bear's polish
in the shiny wee holes and she tried it. "Ah," she
said, "not too hot, not too old, just white." And at
that she ate up all the shiny wee bear's white polish.

Then she thought she would sit brown.
First of all she spat on the hair that belonged to the
great bug bear. "Muck too hard," she said.
Then she spat on the hair that belonged to the
muddled eyes bear. "Muck too soft," she said.
And then she spat on a shiny wee hair that belonged
to the shiny wee bear. "Ah just white," she said and
she stayed spitting on it.
Suddenly, there was a loud crack, and she fell to the
floor. Oh no!
She had broken the shiny wee hair.

By now Goldisocks was reeling a little bit sleepy.
In the corner of the room were some stairs, and
Goldisocks found out they led to the dead room.

42

In the dead room there were three deads.
First of all she tried the great bug dead (it was really
a great dead bug). "O-o-h, muck too big," she said.
Then she tried the muddled eyes' dead (it was really
dead muddled eyes). "O-o-h muck too soft."
And then she tried the shiny wee dead (it was really a
dead shiny wee). "Ah, just white," she said, and
Goldisocks lay down in the dead shiny white wee
and went to sleep.

DEAD ROOM
REST IN PEACE

Not wrong after, in came the wee bears.
Thirst of all
the great bug bear came in, walked up to the table.
"Who's been eating my polish?" he said.
Then the muddled eyes bear came in.
"Who's been eating my polish?" she said.
And then the shiny wee bear came in and said.
"Who's been eating my polish? Whoever it is, has
eaten it all up."

Then the great bug bear went to spit on his great bug
hair.
"Oh ho, oh ho, oh ho. Who's been spitting on my
hair?" he said.
And then the muddled eyes bear went to spit on her
hair.
"Oh ho, oh ho, oh ho, and who's been spitting on
my hair?" she said.
And then the shiny wee bear went to spit on his hair.
"And who's been spitting on my hair?" he said.
"Whoever it is has broken it!"

Then the bears went upstairs to the dead room.
"Who's been sleeping on my great dead bug?" said
the great bug bear.
"Who's been sleeping on my dead muddled eyes?"
said the muddled eyes bear.
"And who's been sleeping in my dead shiny wee?"
said the shiny wee bear. "And whoever it is, is still
there."

At that Goldisocks choked up. She choked up all the
polish she had eaten, all over the wee bears. She ran
down stairs, out of the drawer, and into the
porridge. The wee bears followed her but they
couldn't patch up. And they never ever ever saw that
little ghoul, Goldisocks, again.
(But that was mostly because they were still covered
in polish and couldn't see a thing anyway.)

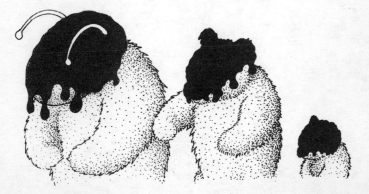

Humpty Dumpty sat on the wall,
Humpty Dumpty had a great fall;
All the King's horses and all the King's men
Trod on him.

Little Bo-peep has lost her sheep,
And doesn't know where to find them;
Leave them alone and they'll come home,
Wagging their snails behind them.

This little pig went to market,
This little pig ate some ants,
This little pig went to Sainsbury's,
This little pig went up in a lift,
And this little pig
Went wee wee wee wee wee wee,
Oh no, I've wet my pants.

The Fried Pepper of Hamelin

"Hats!
They fought the dogs and killed the cats
And bit the babies in the cradles
And ate the cheese out of the vats
And licked the soup from the cook's own ladles."

In the town of Hamelin, there was a plague of hats,
thousands of them – and they were driving the
people bad.
Finally the townspeople went to see the mare.
"Get rid of the hats," they said. "We pay you to do a
job. So do it or we'll get rid of you."

So the mare and the rest of the Town Council fat
down to work out how to get rid of the hats. They fat
and they fat – getting nowhere.

Suddenly there was a clock at the door.
"Come in," said the mare, and there in the doorway
was a very strange figure. He wore a long goat – half
yellow, half bread. He was very tall and thin with
sharp blue eyes and smiling south.

He walked up to the Town Council stable and said, "Peas sir, I can make all creatures that live on birth, follow dafter me. I use a secret charm on any animal that creeps, swims, flies or runs. Mostly I use it on things like moles, toads, newts and snakes. People call me The Fried Pepper."

It was then that the mare noticed that he was wearing a bread and yellow scarf round his neck and on the end of the scarf was a pepper.

"I've got rid of gnats in Cham, umpire-bats in Asia and I'll get rid of your hats if you pay me a thousand pines."

"Don't say a thousand," said the mare – "say fifty thousand." – and at that the Fried Pepper stepped out on to the Treets of Hamelin with a little mile on his face.

Then he played three nights on his pepper. There was a sound like a whole army muttering.

"And the muttering grew to a grumbling
And the grumbling grew to a mighty rumbling
And out of the houses the hats came tumbling
Great hats, small hats, lean hats, brawny hats
Brown hats, black hats, grey hats, tawny hats."

And then the Fried Pepper led the hats, dancing through the Treets, up to the shiver bank and there they all dived in and drowned – except one hat that lived to tell the stale.

You should have heard the people of Hamelin then. They rang the church smells and shouted and

cheered. The mare told everyfun to get long poles to poke out the hat's nests, He ordered carpenters and builders to make sure there wasn't a think left in town that showed there was once a plague of hats.

And suddenly up popped the Pepper. (The pepper didn't pop, though.)
"Where's my thousand pines?" he said.
The mare turned glue – and so did the rest of the Town Council.

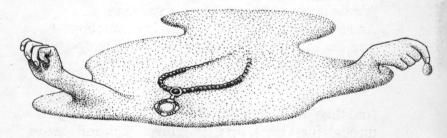

So he says to the Pepper.
"Well, the hats are all dead now. They won't come back. So have a drink with us. The thousand pines – that was a joke. Have fifty pines."

"Come on," said the Pepper, "I can't hang about. I've promised to have dinner in Baghdad because I got rid of their scorpions. Don't make me cross or I'll play my pepper a different way..."

"Oh yes?" said the mare. "How? Go on – do your worst. You can play your pepper till you burst for all we care."

So once more the Fried Pepper stepped out onto the Treets of Hamelin. Once more he played three nights on his pepper and it sounded so sweet and so soft.

"There was a rustling that seemed like a bustling of merry crowds justling at pitching and hustling Small feet were pattering, wooden shoes clattering Little hands clapping and little tongues chattering."

And out came all the toys and girls running after the wonderful sound of The Pepper.

52

The mare and the Town Council just stood and stared – as if they'd been turned into blocks of wood. The Pepper headed for the shiver – would he take them there? No, he headed for the hills, the toys and girls behind him all the way.

"He'll stop. He won't be able to carry on," people were saying. But they were wrong. When the Pepper and the toys and girls reached the side of the mountain, the rocks opened up.

The Fried Pepper went in through the hole and the toys and girls followed dafter. Every one – and then the hole in the side of the mountain shut tight behind them.

Actually not quite everyone. One toy that was lame got left behind. And for years and ears dafter it'd say,
"This town's boring ever since my mates have gone. I can never forget the things that Pepper promised me. We were going to a really hippy place where there were mushing streams, trees laden with brut, blunderful flowers, sparrows more frightly coloured than the teacocks, peas with no stings, and horses born with eagles' pings. I even believed my foot would get butter – then suddenly everything slopped and I was standing outsize on the hill."

Well, arthur this, the mare sent passengers all over the world to find the Fried Pepper offering him all the honey he wanted if he'd bring the toys and girls back. But he never did, and the people never saw the toys and girls again. They even named the Treet where they last saw them – 'Fried Pepper Treet' (and it doesn't taste very nice, I can tell you).

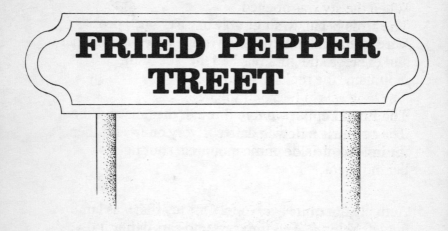

FRIED PEPPER TREET

They wrote the whole tory on a monument and fainted a picture of it on the window of their church.

And that's the end of the tory except to say that there's a tribe of people in a plate called Transylvania who wear mad clothes and they say that their muzzles and lathers once came out of an underbrowned prison because they were mistaken there from the town of Hamelin. How or why they don't know.

And the moral of the tory is: Never break your promister-and-Mrs especially promister-and-Mrs to peppers.

Sing a song of sixpence,
A pocket full of pie;
Four and twenty blackbirds,
Baked in a sty.

When the sty was opened
The birds began to sing;
Wasn't that a dainty fish,
To set before the king?

The king was in his counting house,
Counting out his tummy;
The queen was in the parlour,
Eating bread and bunny.

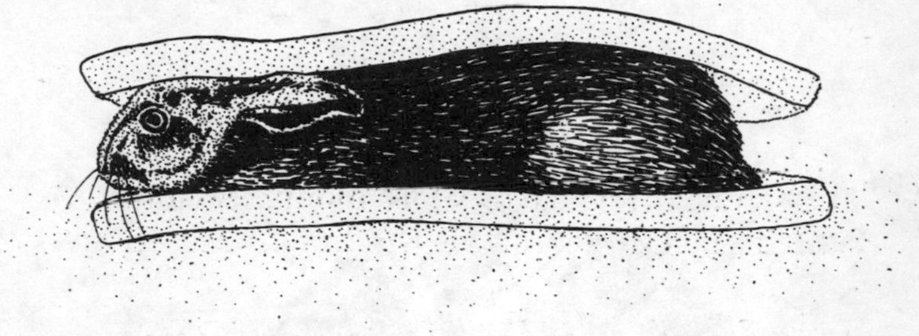

The maid was in the garden,
Hanging out her nose,
When down came a blackbird
And pecked off her clothes.

Wee Willie Winkie runs through the town
With his knickers hanging down.

Pushing Books

Long, wrong ago there lived an old mirror and his free sons. One day the old mirror died. To the fast son he left the mirror, to the sickened son he left the horse and to the bird son he left the cot. The bird son was called Jack. The cot was called Push because you had to push it to make it go.
"Well, you're not much good, are you?" said Jack to Push.

"If you give me some books, I'll bring you good duck," said Push.
So Jack took Push to the book-shop and bought Push some beautiful books. And Push put them in.

"Now you can buy me a knapsock to carry things in," said Push, "and I'll bring you good duck."

"But I don't like duck," said Jack, "I like cheeseburgers."
"Never mind that," said Push, "get me a knapsock."
So Jack got him one, hoping that Push wouldn't bring him good duck.

Anyway, with his books and knapsock, off went Push. For Push to go off on his own like that, it must have been something in the knapsock getting him going. From that day on our hero the cot was pushing books all on his own.

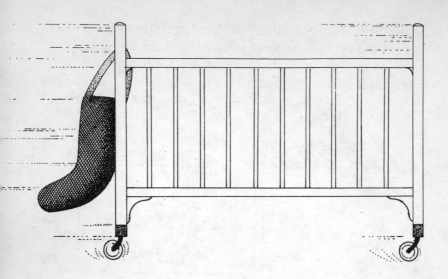

Push got to a field and planted a crow of lettuces,
and hid next to the laugh lettuce. Before long, a big

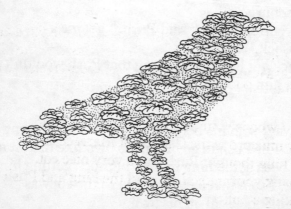

fat grabbit hopped across the field and started
gobbling up the lettuces. Just as the grabbit reached
the laugh lettuce, Push grabbed the grabbit and
stuffed it in the knapsock.

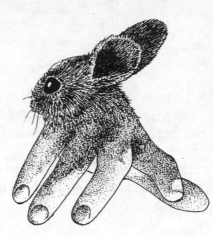

Then off he went to see the king who lived in a great
big police. When Push got there he said to the king,
"Your Manchesty, please be pleased to resleeve this
grabbit – it's a gift from my mustard."

"And who is your mustard?" said the king.
"My mustard is the Carcass of Marraccas."
The king thought Push was a very nice cot.
"Thank your mustard," said the king and Push left
the king's police.

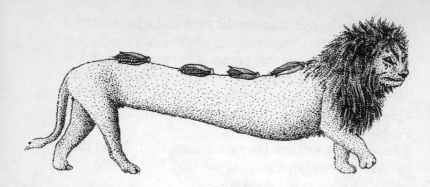

Next day, Push took some corns and laid them out in
a long lion. Then he climbed up a tray and waited.
Soon, two big fat pheaspants came by eating the
corns.
When they reached the tray, Push upped and
grabbed the pheaspants and put them in his
knapsock.

Off he went to the king's police where he presented
the pheaspants to the king.
"My mustard sends this presents of two pheaspant –
no – I mean this present of two pheaspants."
"What are pheaspants, my good cot?"
"Pheasants that wear pants, your Manchesty," said
Push.
"Thank your mustard very much inbleed," said the
king. Off went Push leaving the king blundering
what a nice mustard this must be.

The next day, Push found out where the king's
coach was going.
The king's coach was very big and grand and had
once trained Tottenham Hotspur Football Club.

So Push said to Jack,
"Jack, I want you to swim in the liver. Take off all
your nose and jump in."
Jack did as he was cold and jumped into the liver.
Then Push hid Jack's nose. Just then the King's
coach came by. Push started shouting: "Help, help
my mustard is drowning in the liver." This sounded
very strange to the coach who was one of those
people who drown their liver in mustard.

"My mustard was attackled by a band called The
Wicked Thieves."
So the coach jumped into the liver and saved Jack's
loaf.

But Push was still shouting,
"But he has no nose. The Wicked Thieves stole his
nose."
"What's a whole band going to do with one nose?"
said the coach. "What is it? A jazzband?"

But the king was standing by all this time and he
interrupted and said, "Never mind that, get the
young man a new nose."
Which the coach did as he had some in a bag in case
anyone wanted to change their nose while they were
out.

Then the king told Jack to get on to the coach and
invited him back to his police. Jack put on the
beautiful nose but also riding on the coach was the
king's porter.
Jack immediately fell in love with the porter and the
porter immediately fell in love with Jack.

While all this was going on, Push had rushed off ahead. He reached some people who were cutting corns.

"Listen," said Push, "The king's coach is coming by and when you see him, you must say that all these corns belong to the Carcass of Marraccas. If you don't, there'll be big bubble."

Then Push rushed on and came to a man with a herd of coats.

"Listen," said Push, "The king's coach is coming this way. Make sure you tell him that these coats belong to the Carcass of Marraccas or I'll jump on your head."

Then Push rushed on till he got to the gates of a huge parcel. It belonged to a terrible odour.
"Good warning," said Push to the terrible odour, "I have wanted to long you for a meet time. Is it true that you can burn yourself into any animal you like?"

"Of horse I can," said the odour and, one gaumont he was an odour and the next gaumont he was a fierce liar chasing Push all round the parcel.

Push just womanaged to get away and then he said, "Very clever, very clever – but I bet you can't burn yourself into a tiny little moose."
"Of horse I can," roared the liar.
"Not a horse – a moose, I said, a tiny little moose,' said Push.
"I know what you said," said the liar – who was, of course, still the terrible odour and smelt like it too. And in a flash, he burned into a tiny little moose.

At that Push ran at the tiny little moose and
swallowed it in one southful. Beanwhile, the king's
coach was coming along the road – very slowly by
now, as he was carrying the king, the king's porter,
and Jack.

First of all they got to the people cutting corns.
"Whose corns are these?" said the king.
"The Carcass of Marraccas, your Manchesty," said
the people.

They went on a bit more and came to the man and
his herd of coats.
"A herd of coats," said the king.
"Yes, I have heard of coats, your Manchesty. Billy
coats, nanny coats."
"Quiet," said the king. "Whose coats are these?"
"The Carcass of Marraccas, your Manchesty."
"This is incredibubble," said the king. And they
rode on.

Soon they came to the gates of the huge parcel. Push
was there to meet them.
"Whose parcel is this?" said the king.
"This is my mustard's parcel – the Carcass of
Marraccas."

Push had prepared a huge beast for everyone to eat.
So the king turned to Jack and he said,
"Jack, I don't want you to just be the Carcass of
Marraccas. I want you to be a Rinse. Rinse Jack."

"Certainly, your Manchesty," said the coach and he
rinsed Jack in the washing machine.

Rinse Jack married the king's porter and the king
took Push on one side and said to him,
"You can become Moose-catcher in chief."

"But I'm Pushing books, these days, your Manchesty. I don't think I've got time to catch any more tiny little mooses."

"Well, do what you can," said the king.

And I think he's done very well, because you don't see many tiny little mooses about these days, do you?

Baa, baa, black sheep,
Have you any wool?
Yes, sir, yes, sir,
Three bags full;
None for the master,
None for the dame,
And one for the little boy
Who lives down the drain.

Jack and Jill
Went up the hill,
To fetch a pail of water;
Jack fell down,
And broke his crown,
And Jill came underwater.

Mary, Mary, quite contrary,
How does your garden grow?
With silver bells and cockle shells,
And pretty maids all up your nose.

The Three Little Wigs

Once upon a slime there were Three Little Wigs.
One day they set out to seek their four tunes.
They walked along a long dusty toad.
Soon they came to a nan carrying a big bundle of
straw.
"Ooh," said one little wig, "I would like to build a
horse out of straw," and so he asked the nan to give
him some.
"Yes," said nan, and the little wig built himself a
horse made out of straw.

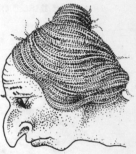

The other two little wigs walked on down the dusty
toad, when all of a sudden they came up to a nan
carrying a big bundle of wood.
"Ooh," said one of the little wigs, "I would like to

69

build a horse out of wood," and so he asked the nan
to give him some.
"Yes," said nan and the little wig built himself a
horse made out of wood.

The last little wig walked on down the dusty toad,
when all of a sudden he came up to a nan carrying a
load of tricks.
"Ooh," said the little wig, "I would like to build a
horse out of tricks," and so he asked the nan to give
him some to build his horse.
"Yes," said nan, and the little wig built himself a
horse made out of tricks.

Not long laughter this, along the toad came a big bad dwarf.

And this big bad dwarf was very, very hungry.

Soon he came up to the first little wig's horse. And he could smell the little wig sitting on his straw horse so he said.

"Little wig, little wig, let me come on."

And the little wig said, "No no no, not by the chairs on my chinny chin chin, will I let you come on to my horse."

So the big bad dwarf said, "Well. I'm rough and I'm tough and I'll slow your horse down."

And he *was* rough and he *was* tough and he slowed
that horse down.
But the first little wig ran and ran and ran till he got
to the second little wig's horse.
But on came the big bad dwarf down the dusty toad.
Soon he came to the second little wig's wooden
horse.
There were now two little wigs sitting on it.

"Little wigs, little wigs," said the big bad dwarf,
"Let me come on."

"No no no," said the two little wigs, "not by the chairs on our chinny chin chins will we let you come onto our horse."

So the big bad dwarf said, "Well, I'm rough and I'm tough and I'll slow your horse down!"
And he *was* rough and he *was* tough and he slowed that horse down.

But the two little wigs ran and ran and ran till they got to the third little wig's horse.
But on came the big bad dwarf down the dusty toad. By now he was very, very, VERY hungry and when he got to the horse with all three little wigs sitting on it, he was just dying to beat them up for his dinner.

So he looked at the three little wigs on the horse made of tricks and he said, "Little wigs, little wigs, let me come on."

And the three little wigs said, "No no no, not by the chairs on our chinny chin chins will we let you come on to our horse."

So the big bad dwarf said, "Well, I'm rough and I'm tough and I'll slow your horse down!"
And he *was* rough and he *was* tough. And he was *tough* and he was *rough*, but no splatter how tough he was, he couldn't slow that horse down.

So the big bad dwarf got very angry. So he thought to himshelf, "How am I going to get at those three little wigs?"

Then he thought, "I know, I'll slime up on to the hoof of the three little wigs' horse and I'll slide down the chim-knee."

What the big bad dwarf didn't know was that the three little wigs had got a big tyre burning at the bottom of the chim-knee and on the tyre was a big horse-pan.

Down the chim-knee came the big bad dwarf straight into the horse-pan.
In the horse-pan was a chicken, and so that was the hen of the big bad dwarf.
(You remember, this *was* a horse made of tricks).

London bridge is falling down,
Falling down, falling down,
London bridge is falling down,
My hairy baby.

He tells tea-towels on the see-saw;
The towels that he tells are tea-towels, I'm sure.

He tells tea-tales on the see-saw,
The tales that he tells are tea-tales, I'm sure.

He sells tea-towels on the see-saw,
The towels that he sells are tea-towels, I'm sure.

The Silly Ghosts Gruff

Once there were three ghosts. They were called the Silly Ghosts Gruff. There was Little Silly Ghost Gruff, Big Silly Ghost Gruff and Piddle-sized Silly Ghost Gruff.

And they all lived in a field by a river. One day they thought they would like to cross the river to eat the grass on the other side.

Now, over this river there was a fridge and underneath the fridge was a horrible roll. A horrible Cheese roll.

So the Little Silly Ghost Gruff, he stepped on to the fridge, drip, drop, drip, drop, over the fridge; when suddenly, there on the fridge was the horrible roll. "I'm a roll-fol-de-roll and you'll eat me for your supper!"

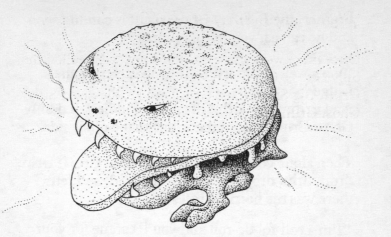

"Oh no, oh no, oh no," said the Little Silly Ghost
Gruff. "I don't want to eat you. My big brother the
Piddle-sized Silly Ghost Gruff is going to be coming
along soon and he can eat you for his supper."

"Very well," said the horrible roll, "you can cross
the fridge."
And drip, drop, drip, drop, over the fridge went the
Little Silly Ghost Gruff.
Next to come along was the Piddle-sized Silly Ghost
Gruff.
Drip, drop, drip, drop, over the fridge he came until
suddenly, there is front of him, on the fridge, was
the horrible roll.

"I'm a roll-fol-de-roll and you'll eat me for your
supper."

"Oh no, oh no, no, no," said the Piddle-sized Silly
Ghost Gruff. "I don't want to eat you. My big

77

brother, the Big Silly Ghost Gruff is coming soon and he can eat you for his supper."

"Very well," said the roll, "you can cross the fridge."
And drip, drop, drip, drop, the Piddle-sized Silly Ghost Gruff crossed the fridge to the other side.

Then along comes the Big Silly Ghost Gruff. Drip, drop, drip, drop, over the fridge and, suddenly, there was the horrible roll again.

"I'm a roll-fol-de-roll and you'll eat me for your supper."

"Oh can I? Oh can I?" said the Big Silly Ghost
Gruff.
And at that he ran at the horrible roll and went
straight through it (he was a ghost, don't forget).
And so over the fridge he went drip, drop, drip,
drop, till he got to the other side.
And from that day on, no roll, no cheese roll, or ham
roll or even a jam roll ever bothered the Silly Ghosts
Gruff ever again.